Community Helpers

My Visit to the Dentist

David Lee

illustrated by
Anita Morra

PowerKiDS
press

New York

Published in 2017 by The Rosen Publishing Group, Inc.
29 East 21st Street, New York, NY 10010

First Edition

Managing Editor: Nathalie Beullens-Maoui
Editor: Caitie McAneney
Book Design: Michael Flynn
Illustrator: Anita Morra

Library of Congress Cataloging-in-Publication Data

Names: Lee, David, 1990- author.
Title: My visit to the dentist / David Lee.
Description: New York : PowerKids Press, [2017] | Series: Community helpers |
  Includes index.
Identifiers: LCCN 2016027413| ISBN 9781499427042 (pbk. book) | ISBN
  9781499427059 (6 pack) | ISBN 9781499430301 (library bound book)
Subjects: LCSH: Dentistry–Juvenile literature. | Teeth–Care and
  hygiene–Juvenile literature.
Classification: LCC RK63 .L44 2017 | DDC 617.6–dc23
LC record available at https://lccn.loc.gov/2016027413

Manufactured in the United States of America

CPSIA Compliance Information: Batch #BW17PK: For Further Information contact Rosen Publishing, New York, New York at 1-800-237-9932

Contents

It's time to get my teeth cleaned.

4

I go to the dentist.

The dentist sits next to me.

The dentist turns on a
bright light.

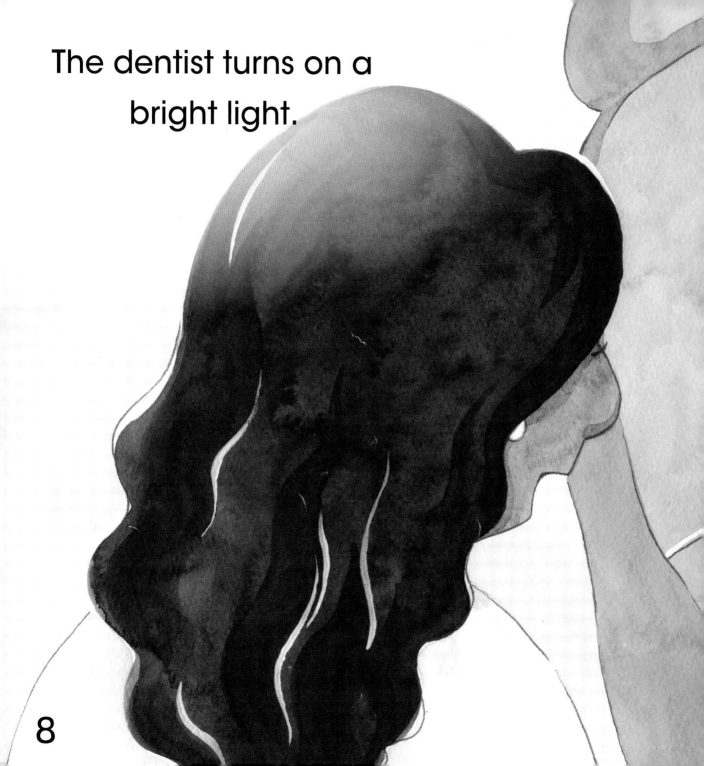

She looks in my mouth.

Say ahhh!

9

The dentist says my teeth are called baby teeth.

Some day I will grow new ones.

The dentist says my teeth look healthy.

I take care of them!

13

The dentist shows me how
to floss my teeth.

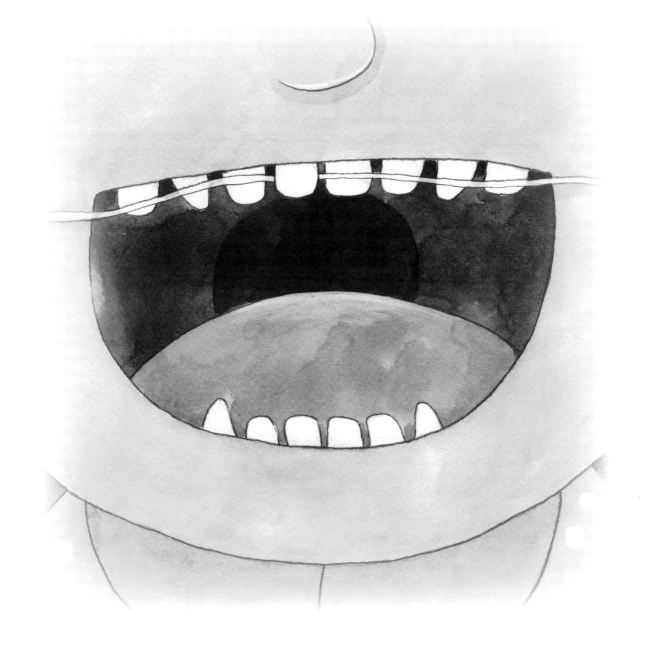

Floss is like a string.

The dentist shows me how
to brush my teeth.

I'm good at this already!

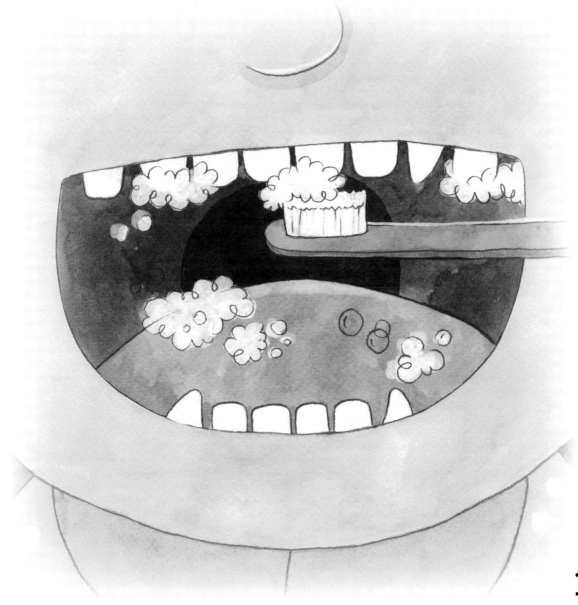

All done!

18

The dentist tells me my teeth are like new.

19

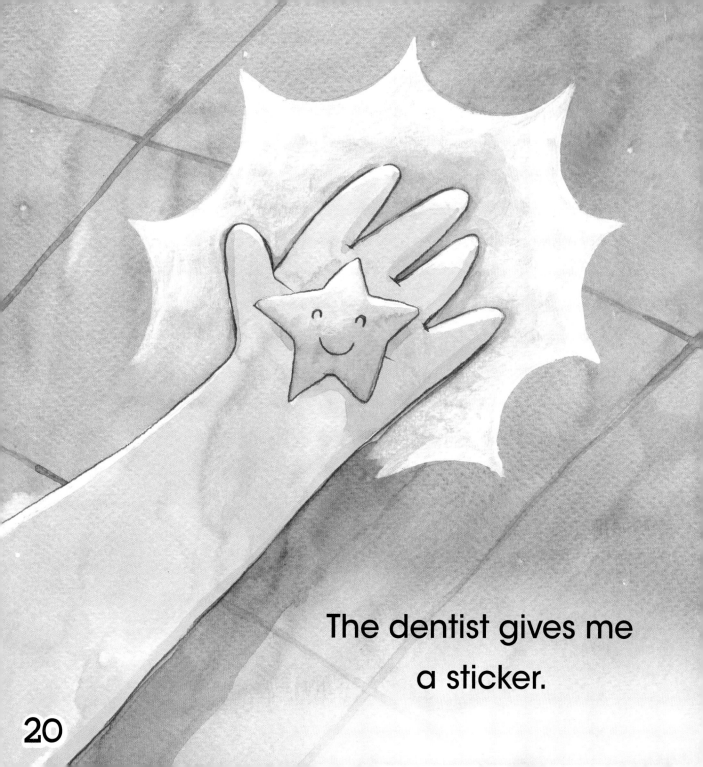

The dentist gives me
a sticker.

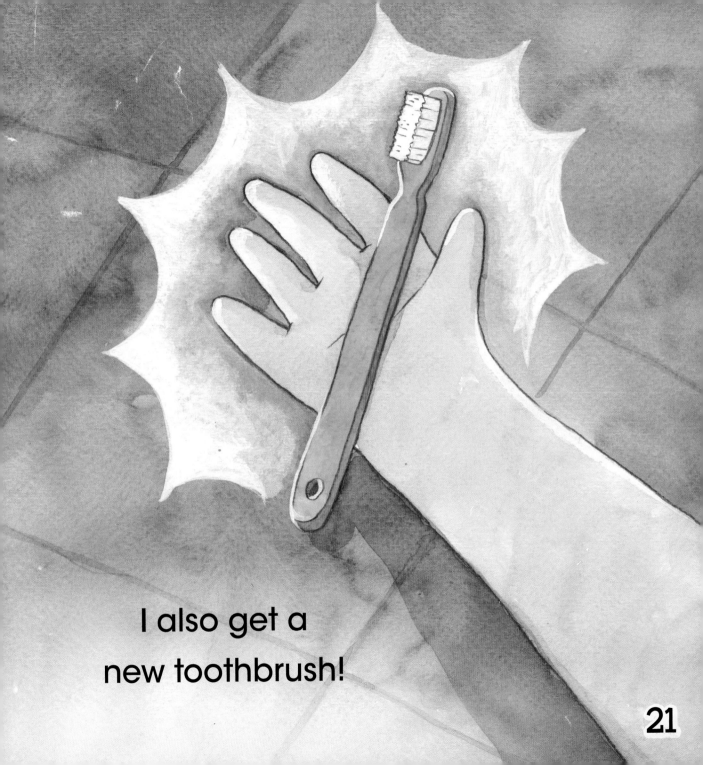

I also get a
new toothbrush!

It's important to
have healthy teeth.

I love going to the dentist!

23

Words to Know

floss

teeth

toothbrush

Index

24